# HOCKEY WAS BENNY'S LIFE...

"Who's got the puck?" Benny asked. He glared at them. "Where is that piece of licorice stick we used for the last game?"

Peppy shifted from one foot to the other.

"I think Peppy has something to tell you," said Figaro.

"Well, out with it," Benny demanded.

"I ate it," Peppy said miserably. He stared down at the ice and chipped at it with his stick. "I was hungry this morning."

"Ate the puck!" screamed Benny the Bullet. "Have you no respect?"

NELSON NOVELS

# MICE AT CENTRE ICE

ESTELLE SALATA

**NELSON** CANADA

**Series Editor** Meguido Zola
**Illustrations** Malcolm Collett, Canamerica
               Entertainment Corp.
**Design** David Taylor/Taylor/Levkoe Associates
**Editors** Elma Schemenauer, Peggy Foy
**Typesetting** Trigraph Inc.
**Printing** Best Gagné Book Manufacturers

*Zamboni is a registered trade mark of
 Frank J. Zamboni & Co. Ltd.

Published in 1984 by
Nelson Canada,
A Division of International Thomson Limited
1120 Birchmount Road
Scarborough, Ontario
M1K 5G4

ISBN 0-17-602086-1

**Canadian Cataloguing in Publication Data**

Salata, Estelle.
  Mice at centre ice

ISBN 0-17-602086-1

1. Mice - Juvenile fiction. 2. Rats - Juvenile fiction.
I. Title.

PS8587.A42M52 1984     jC813'.54     C83-099265-0
PZ10.3.S24Mi 1984

Printed and bound in Canada

    19 20 21 22 23 24 25 BBM 0 9 8 7

To Ben, Michael, Paula, Kathy, and Mark

# Table of Contents

# Chapter One

# HOCKEY NIGHT

I T WAS Saturday night at the Montreal Forum. The third period of the hockey game was almost over. Benny the Bullet's nose twitched. His feet itched to be out on the ice. He wished he were playing for the Cheddar Cup in the Mouse Hockey League, instead of watching the Stanley Cup playoffs.

Peppy la Pierre and Figaro the Flyer lounged against the boards beneath the box seats. That was one thing, Benny thought. He and the other mice had the best seats in the house. Saturday night hockey crowds ordered the best food money could buy—potato chips, hot dogs, and buttered popcorn.

Just then the right winger made a slap shot from the blue line. It caught the goalie off guard. The red light flashed on. It was the winning goal and the crowd went wild. It was a wonder the people didn't trample him and the other mice

underfoot, Benny thought angrily. He glanced up at the clock. There were only a few seconds left in the game.

"What a dumb way to score a goal!" Benny stood up. "No passing. No neat stick handling. No class. Period."

Peppy la Pierre dug into a bag of peanuts someone had dropped on the floor. Benny kicked the bag away from him.

"What did you do that for?" Peppy cried.

"You've had enough." Figaro cleaned his whiskers.

"I've seen enough of this game," said Benny. "We have to get into shape for our own hockey game."

"What's wrong with me?" asked Peppy. "I'm in good shape. I can play hockey."

"You'll never be able to skate for the Cheddar Cup," Benny poked Peppy in the stomach. "You're beginning to look like a fat cat."

"The Cheddar Cup?" Figaro frowned. "I've never heard of that opera. Is it new?"

"Never heard of the Cheddar Cup!" Benny glared at him. He jerked his thumb at the exit. "Come on. Let's get out of here before someone makes minced mouse out of us."

He dodged a spike heel and a pair of sneakers, and led the way past hundreds of pairs of shoes. The three mice darted and dodged their way to their locker room. The other locker room was off limits to the mice. The Rink Rats lived there. Peppy, Figaro, and Benny scurried through the hole in the baseboard and headed for their favourite place.

In the dressing room, Peppy stretched out on an old goalie pad. The pad had been made by the legendary Pops Kinesky. Figaro sat inside his special hockey glove. Benny stood on the bench.

"What's this about the Cheddar Cup, Benny?" asked Figaro. "Are we going to the opera?" He hummed a few bars from *Rigoletto*.

Benny sighed. Figaro had this thing about opera. He had come over to the Forum all the way from Place des Arts, the concert hall in Montreal.

"We're going to organize our own hockey teams again," Benny told Figaro and Peppy. "We can play better than those professional hockey players. It's time to revive the old MHL."

"I thought we only played for fun," said Peppy. "We don't *have* the Cheddar Cup."

Benny sat down on the bench.

"We *have* only been playing for fun up until now," he explained. "Soon, we'll play for keeps again."

Every night after the National Hockey League game, the Montreal Canadiens and their opponents left the ice. The crowds went home and the ice was empty. Then Benny, Peppy, and Figaro played shinny by themselves. Sometimes some of the other mice at the Forum joined them. They just got out there on the ice to score as many goals as they could, and to hog the puck as much as possible.

"A long time ago," Benny told Figaro, and Peppy nodded knowingly, "the mice had a proper league—the Mouse Hockey League. The teams played in the MHL for the Cheddar Cup. My grandfather told me about the good old days. He played for the Cup the last time it was ever seen."

"What happened?" asked Figaro. Peppy rolled over on his pudgy tummy and put his chin in his paws.

"The night of the big game," Benny

began, "my grandfather's team won against the team from the Gardens. The Cheddar Cup was the prize. They rolled it out onto the ice. It took fifty mice or more to move it. Then, a terrible thing happened."

Benny certainly had Peppy and Figaro's attention now. He could have heard a marshmallow drop.

"The Rink Rats stole the Cheddar Cup right from under their noses," he went on. "They skated out onto the ice and just grabbed the Cup. My grandfather and his teammates tried to stop them, but they weren't strong enough. The Rink Rats are rough and tough."

"Where is the Cup?" asked Figaro.

"They keep it in their secret room," Benny told him. He stood up and paced back and forth across the bench. "They keep the Cheddar Cup behind the floorboards. No one has ever dared to get it back. It's too dangerous."

He shuddered.

"Why not?" demanded Peppy. He jumped up and down. "It's our Cup. It belongs to us."

The vision of an entire cup made of cheese was too much for Peppy, thought

Benny. It made a bag of peanuts look like a cracker without the cheese. Peppy turned somersaults on the goalie pad.

"The Cheddar Cup is so old and so sacred that no mouse can remember its beginnings," Benny said in a solemn voice. "They say it was made long ago by the Master Mouse Moulder, an artist named Raphaela."

The three mice crossed their hearts.

"But you said it was made of cheese," Peppy protested. "And you *know* how I love cheese."

"This is no ordinary cup," said Benny. "It is made of the finest gourmet cheese in the world. It was aged in a wooden cask and sealed in a special wax. They say that those who have eaten even one bite are never the same again."

"We should definitely have it back," Peppy announced.

"What are we going to do, Benny?" asked Figaro.

"Steal it back," Benny whispered hoarsely. "I have a plan. It involves a dangerous mission. Listen!"

## Chapter Two

# TRAPPED

THE locker room was quiet and cosy. It smelled of leather and damp sweaters and worn socks. An old red sweater with blue and white stripes hung on a hook in the corner. Hockey pucks, sticks, a forgotten skateboard, and a basketball were piled in a corner. This had been home for as long as Benny could remember. It smelled of hockey.

"What's the good of a Cup made of cheese if you can't eat it?" Peppy interrupted Benny's thoughts. "What's the point of playing for something that you can just look at?"

"No one can *eat* the real Cheddar Cup," explained Benny. "The mice from the Forum and the Great Outdoors used to come and fill the Cup to the top with the finest cheese in the world. It was cheese they had been saving on their travels. Edam, Gouda, Brie, Camembert, Roquefort, Cheddar...."

"You understand, don't you?" Benny went on. 'It's the principle that counts. The Cheddar Cup stands for something. Not even the Rink Rats would eat it. At least, I don't think they would. They haven't eaten it yet."

"I *do* understand," said Figaro. "The Cup is sacred like the Holy Grail or the Golden Fleece."

"Exactly!" Benny replied. "That's why we fill the Cup with cheese and eat that instead. But first things first. We have to get the Cheddar Cup back before we can play hockey for it. Are you with me?"

"Of course." Figaro got to his feet at once. "It is a noble cause." Then he became thoughtful. "But tell me, Benny, who are our opponents? Surely we don't just play each other for the Cup?"

"In the old days," Benny explained, "the League was country-wide. The MHL players would hide inside the gear of the NHL teams and travel the land. After every NHL game, an exactly parallel MHL match would follow. Montreal against Toronto; Winnipeg against Edmonton, and so on. My grandfather's team won the most—at least, that's the way he tells it." Benny's voice trailed off as, all at once, the three mice sensed danger.

Suddenly the bench, hockey pads, gloves, and other equipment bounced up and down. The clatter of skate blades thundered down the steps to the locker room. The sound sent cold shivers of fear up Benny's spine. He had skate blade nightmares almost every night.

"Run for your lives!" cried Figaro.

He scurried for the hole in the baseboards, with Peppy and Benny behind him. They made it inside before the Canadiens came into the locker room. The huge human players laughed and joked with one another, faces marked with cuts and bruises. Their wet uniforms clung to their bodies.

The mice curled up in a snug little threesome. While they waited for the hockey players to leave, Benny told of the glorious days of the Cheddar Cup.

"It was in my grandfather's time that the Rink Rats stole it," Benny said fiercely. "And it will be in my time that we get it back. I'd rather be a dead hero than a live coward."

Peppy and Figaro swallowed hard and nodded.

"No one has the heart to play in the MHL any more," Benny concluded. "Some of us young mice began to play hockey just for fun once again. But now is the time to bring the Cheddar Cup back to its rightful place."

"When do we start?" Peppy wanted to know.

"Let's not rush into anything." Figaro tweaked his whiskers nervously. "We should think things through."

"Maybe we should investigate," Peppy suggested.

"Good idea," Benny said. "Let's go."

Noiselessly they crept along the tunnel behind the baseboards of the Visiting Team's dressing room. Luckily, the Rink Rats didn't notice anything.

The Rats were sitting around the locker room as if they owned the place, finishing a submarine sandwich. Big Boris Ringsky, the biggest rat of them all, sat in the middle of the ring. He was telling the others about the Cheddar Cup. He puffed on a ragged cigar butt.

"Oh, yeah!" he said with a knowing grin. "That was *some* night. My grandfather told me all about it. It's just as if it had been myself, Big Boris Ringsky the

Third, who scored the winning goal against the Mice. My grandfather told us that story every morning before we went to bed. The Mice had tied the game at 1-all. There were fewer than sixty seconds to play before going into overtime. Then my grandfather stole the puck right out from under the twitching little nose of the Bullet himself and scored the winning goal."

Big Boris settled back on an old duffle bag and crossed his scrawny legs. He took a long drag on the cigar butt.

Benny's ears burned and his nose twitched with anger. "He's telling it all wrong!" he whispered to Peppy and Figaro. "We won the Cup fair and square. The Rink Rats stole it! They didn't win it."

Just then Big Boris looked slowly around the room. He sniffed at the air.

"I smell something funny." His nose tweaked in all directions. He stopped when he was facing the three friends' hideout. They huddled in their spot, hidden by an old megaphone.

"I smell mouse," said a tough-looking rat with a scarred face.

The rats were all shifting about restlessly, looking around with suspicion. For a moment, the mice froze. Then Benny made a dash for a tiny hole he saw at the far end of the room, followed by Figaro and Peppy.

"There they go!" cried Big Boris. "After them!"

Old Scarface obeyed. He raced after Benny and the others, but stopped short outside the hole. It was too small for a rat.

"Ah, let them go," said Big Boris. He jammed the cigar butt back into his mouth. "They're only mice."

"We gave them a scare, Boss," said Old Scarface. He laughed hoarsely. "They won't be back."

Big Boris settled back on his duffle bag. He grunted.

"At least they didn't find out where the Cheddar Cup is hidden," he said.

Benny's ears perked up as he strained to listen. The Cheddar Cup! The Rats still had it! His heart pounded with excitement.

"Where is it?" asked Old Scarface. "And why haven't we eaten it?"

"We're saving it for hard times," said Big Boris. He stuttered and sounded embarrassed. "There's talk of boarding up the Forum and building a new arena somewhere else. Where would we get our food without hockey players and fans? We'd starve to death, or have to live in the sewers."

Big Boris's voice dropped to a whisper. The other rats gathered close and listened.

"The Cheddar Cup is sealed in special wax," he said. "It will never go bad. We keep it in a secret room in there." He jerked his head towards the mouse hole. "No human being has used that room in years. The old closet has been boarded up for good."

The mice didn't wait to hear another word. They were so close to the Cheddar Cup they could almost smell it. Benny led the way through another tunnel behind the locker room. Big Boris had said the Cup was in a small room, an old closet. The voices of the Rink Rats rumbled as they laughed and talked and told tall tales about their wonderful deeds of the past.

Benny, Figaro, and Peppy scampered along the cold stones. Benny stopped to inspect every opening in the wall. Finally they came to a low door with a large hole at the bottom. Benny hurried through to the other side. The others followed.

The room was small and empty. A shaft of light shone through from a crack in the ceiling. Their eyes followed the beam of light.

There in front of them stood the Cheddar Cup! It was exactly like the Stanley Cup. Instead of silver, though, the bright orange cheddar shone with a waxy glow more beautiful than any silver or gold. It was magnificent. It stood on a small wooden pedestal made from a bannister.

"It rightfully belongs to us!" Benny said. He and the others took a closer look.

Engraved around the bottom tier were tiny letters with the names of the Most Valuable Players and the winning teams. Benny read the name of his grandfather, "Benny the Bullet the First." And he was Benny the Bullet the Third. How proud he was to bear his grandfather's name! Somehow, he had to live up to that name. "I must get the Cup back at any cost!" he declared.

"And we'll help you," the others agreed. They tried to move the Cup.

They pushed and shoved. They huffed and puffed. But nothing happened.

Then a noise startled them. They turned to look.

Big Boris glared down at Benny.

"So you've found the Cheddar Cup, have you?" He couldn't see the other two mice, hidden by the Cup. He grabbed Benny by the scruff of the neck and shook him. "Well, it won't do you any good, you little runt. It's ours now and we're going to keep it. We won it in a hockey game."

"No, you didn't," Benny blurted out. "You stole it."

"Guards!" shouted Big Boris.

Two small rats with shifty eyes scurried into the room through a large hole at the rear.

"Yes, Boss." They saluted.

"From now on," ordered Big Boris, "I want twenty-four hour guard duty on the Cheddar Cup. Otherwise, this little squirt will bring his friends here and eat it. Right through the centre."

Benny was shocked. Eat the Cheddar Cup!

"Let go of me!" he demanded. "We challenge the Rink Rats to play hockey for the Cup. We want to win it back—not steal it."

"*You* play the Rink Rats?" Big Boris sneered. "You always were too big for your hockey britches. Well, if you want the Cup, come and get it. Anytime." Then Boris laughed. His laugh sent cold chills down Benny's spine.

With that, he let go of Benny, snapped his fingers at the guards, and swaggered out of the room.

## Chapter Three

# NEVER VENTURE! NEVER WIN!

**B**ACK in the mouse locker room, Benny rummaged around until he found an old hockey program. He and the other mice sat within the warm comfortable circle of light as he sketched a map on the back of the program.

"We are going to heist the Cheddar Cup from the secret room and bring it back here," Benny announced. "Then we'll ask all the mouse hockey players to come here and play for the Cup. It will be just like the good old days when my grandfather played for the great Mouse Hockey League."

"Heist the Cup from under the Rink Rats' noses?" Peppy asked. "I'd rather play them for it. Fair and square."

"I suggested that to Big Boris," said Benny. "But he laughed and told me to 'come and get it.' Well, that's exactly what we're going to do.

"Here is the floor plan of the tunnels in the Forum," Benny went on. He pointed at the map. "They connect our locker room to the Rink Rats' locker room." On the sketch, he quickly traced the route. "First, we have to get past the Rink Rats in their own locker room without being seen."

"Hmmm," Figaro mused. "This sounds like grand opera."

"It's simple," Benny told him. "First, we approach the guardians of the Cup."

"What guardians?" Peppy asked. "You didn't mention anything about guardians before."

"A minor matter," Benny said calmly. "They're just a couple of scrawny old rats who have seen better days."

Figaro looked doubtful. "But how will we ever move it?" he asked.

Benny looked around. In the corner lay a forgotten pile of equipment. He walked over to the abandoned skateboard and leaned against it. The wheels flew out from under him and he fell over. Nevertheless, he was jubilant.

The skateboard was perfect. It wasn't too heavy for the mice to handle together. A little touch and it moved by itself. It would be easy to steer the Cup on wheels through the tunnels. All they had to do was get rid of the two guards.

"This is it, team." Benny tapped the skateboard. "This is the cart that will bring our Cheddar Cup home safely."

"A modern Trojan horse," said Figaro. "A good plan, captain."

Peppy was beside himself with excitement.

"Well, what are we waiting for?" he demanded. He turned a somersault.

"Tomorrow night during the second NHL playoff game," Benny said. "We'll set our plan in motion then."

"Never venture, never win!" said Peppy la Pierre. "That's our motto."

# Chapter Four

# SHINNY

**B**EFORE practice that night, Benny tacked a sign over the knothole in the snack bar:

WANTED
Mouse Hockey Players for the
MOUSE HOCKEY LEAGUE
PRACTICE: Tomorrow at 1:00 A.M. Sharp.

"There," he said to Figaro and Peppy. "That should bring in some good players."

"I'll put that in the *Mouse Hockey News*," said a female voice behind him.

Benny turned. It was Anne Marie, one of the three white mice who lived up in the broadcast booth. Raphaela, the artist, and Mizzy Mouse, the announcer who broadcast the MHL games, were with her.

"We've been watching you practise," said Raphaela. She had sketched Figaro's profile on a scrap of paper, trying to find his good side.

"I can't wait to broadcast the game," said Mizzy Mouse as she pirouetted on the ice.

"The more publicity the better," said Benny.

"You can stay and practise with us if you want," Peppy said to Mizzy Mouse.

"Our pleasure," said Figaro with a sweeping bow.

"Thanks," said one of the white mice, "but we're too busy. We have a paper to put out."

"See you at the game," said Anne Marie. She left a copy of the *Mouse Hockey News* for Benny, Figaro, and Peppy to read.

"Now, let's practise before bed," said Benny, when the three white mice had gone back to the broadcast booth. "We don't want to get too sluggish."

They went to fetch their equipment, and then hurried to the ice. Peppy pulled his goalie mask down over his face until only his eyes, nose, and mouth showed. The mask had been made from a finger of a moth-eaten woollen glove.

Benny would rather play shinny than anything else in the world. He loved the mad scramble for the puck with no holds barred. He loved the feel of the puck cradled against his stick as he broke away and sped across the ice. He loved the wind against his ears and the wild feeling of triumph as he deked Peppy to the right or to the left before sliding the puck into the net right under his nose. In shinny it was each mouse for himself and let the best mouse win.

Benny pulled on red plastic skates with gold safety pin blades. Then came his shining silver helmet made from the tip of a panatella cigar case. The three mice wore matching red, blue, and white sweaters.

They stepped out onto the ice for the warm-up and skated around in circles to get the feel of the ice.

"The ice is slow tonight," Benny said. He dulled his blades on the boards.

They marked out their own regulation-sized rink. Peppy skated back and forth and scraped the ice in the goal with his skates. Benny inspected his two teammates.

"Look at your hockey sticks," he said. "They're a disgrace. Popsicle sticks taped together."

"But captain," Figaro protested, "this

is my lucky stick. It's got a good lie."

"Who's got the puck?" Benny asked. He glared at them. "Where is that piece of licorice stick we used for the last game?"

Peppy shifted from one foot to the other.

"I think Peppy has something to tell you," said Figaro.

"Well, out with it," Benny demanded.

"I ate it," Peppy said miserably. He stared down at the ice and chipped at it with his stick. "I was hungry this morning."

"Ate the puck!" screamed Benny the Bullet. "Have you no respect?"

Figaro took off in search of another puck. "Toreador-a, don't spit on the floor," he sang as he skated. "Use the cuspidor, that's what it's for." Figaro skated back a few moments later with a black button.

Benny tested the button against his stick blade and nodded grudgingly. "Should be rubber," he muttered. "Or licorice."

Figaro placed the new puck in the small red circle within the face-off zone.

"First we'll practise rushes," said

Benny. "One on one. Try to get around me and nail me first. I'll try and nail you, too."

"Let's go!" Figaro leaned forward, his stick across his knees, waiting.

Benny broke loose with the puck and streaked across the ice. Figaro took after him and headed him off. He poked and stabbed at the puck. Benny stick handled around him. A breakaway! Figaro charged from behind. He sprawled full length on the ice, poked his stick in front of Benny, and knocked the puck away. Benny tripped over the stick and belly-flopped to the ice. The puck dribbled towards the net slowly. Peppy stepped out and kicked it away.

Benny and Figaro skidded into the goalpost, head first. They hit the corner of the net full speed.

Benny struggled to his feet and shook his head.

"You can't do that, Figaro," he screamed.

"Why not?" answered Figaro.

"Tripping," snapped Benny the Bullet. "That's why."

"I just saw one of the players do it tonight," said Figaro. "He got away with it."

Benny leaned on his stick.

"That's because the NHL referees are just about blind," he explained. "Didn't you hear the crowd chant 'Three Blind Mice?' Our officials in the Mouse Hockey League are sharp. We won't be able to get away with anything. They'll call it as they see it."

The mice practised a few more rushes, dekes, and slap shots from the blue line.

The Forum was quiet except for the scraping sound of blades on ice and the swish of the button as it skimmed towards the net. Benny felt his muscles begin to ache. It was a good feeling. He and the other mice needed a few more shots on goal before they would be ready for the MHL.

Suddenly loud laughter sounded from the seating section. Benny looked up into the empty stands. But the stands weren't quite empty. Big Boris and three other Rink Rats sprawled in the box seats, eating a banana and cleaning out the bottoms of popcorn boxes.

"Look at that, boys," called Big Boris. "Those little squirts think they can get the Cheddar Cup back from *us* in a hockey game."

He roared with laughter. The others laughed even louder.

Benny's blood boiled.

He stamped his foot, forgetting he was wearing skates. His feet flew out from under him and he landed on the seat of his pants. Quickly he stood up and dusted himself off. He shook his fist at Big Boris.

"We *will* get it back," he shouted, "one way or another. The Cup belongs to us."

"Try and prove it," sneered Big Boris. He stood up and flipped the banana peel onto the ice. It landed behind Figaro, who was practising figure eights backwards. Figaro backed into the peel and did a double flip. He lay still on the ice. Benny and Peppy rushed over.

"Are you all right, Fig?" asked Benny.

*"Mon Dieu!* Speak to us," Peppy begged.

"I can't," murmured Figaro. Slowly he opened one eye and then the other. He rubbed his side. "Just a few bruises. No broken bones."

Figaro struggled to a sitting position. The others helped him to his feet. There was another loud burst of laughter from the stands.

"Challenge us to the Cheddar Cup, will

you?" Big Boris taunted. "Maybe we *will* give you a chance to try and win it back after all." He doubled over, holding his sides. His blood-curdling laughter echoed through the huge building.

"It's our Cup," Benny whispered fiercely. "We're not going to wait to win it back from the Rats. We're going to heist it! I can hardly wait till tomorrow night."

## Chapter Five

# THE SKATEBOARD

THE next day Benny, Figaro, and Peppy worked hard. Figaro had figured out the size of the hole in the baseboard to see if the skateboard would fit. The hole was too small. It took most of the day for the mice to gnaw out the opening until it was big enough. They had to get the skateboard through to the tunnel behind the locker room.

"What if the NHL player wants his skateboard?" asked Peppy. "Sometimes he takes it outside before practice."

"We'll have to take that chance," Benny said. His nose twitched as it always did when he was nervous and excited.

There was nothing left to do except wait until game time. Peppy bedded down in a goalie pad. Figaro curled up on a helmet lined with soft material. Benny slept restlessly for the remainder of the day in a Kleenex box. Under the circumstances it was quite comfortable.

Later that night, the mice sat in the Waiting Room while the Montreal Canadiens dressed for the Stanley Cup playoff game. Benny was as jumpy as a goalie in a tie game. The noise of thousands of people coming into the Forum thundered overhead. Feet stomped. Voices laughed and talked. The music from the great organ swelled. Usually, these noises filled Benny with excitement. Tonight, he could think of nothing except the Cheddar Cup.

"'One Fine Day' from *Madame Butterfly*," said Figaro. "Puccini. It's a good omen."

"What's that about butterflies?" Peppy whispered, glancing around.

"That's what the organist is playing," Figaro explained.

Benny the Bullet glared at him fiercely.

"Sorry, Benny," Figaro said, shifting about uncomfortably. "I don't mean to upset you. It's just that I find opera so soothing in times of stress. It calms me down when I'm upset."

"I'll calm you down," Benny answered. "You should be going over our plan, not blabbing about opera."

At last the locker room was empty.

From above, Benny heard the strains of the National Anthem and then the soaring voice of the soloist. She sang the anthem first in French and then in English. The crowd roared when she had finished.

"The big game is just beginning," said Benny. "I hate to miss the playoffs, but our plan is more important."

It was time to go into action. With the noise overhead, the Rink Rats would never hear the roll of the skateboard through the tunnel.

"Zero hour, team," Benny said. "Let's go!"

Benny led the others to the skateboard and shoved. It coasted easily along the wooden floorboards. Suddenly the wheels stopped turning. Benny and Figaro bent low, shoulder to shoulder, pushing as hard as they could.

"It's no use," Benny gasped. He stopped to catch his breath. "It won't budge."

Then he saw what was making the skateboard so heavy. For a joke, Peppy had stretched himself out on top of it. He was whistling cheerily.

Benny jumped up on the skateboard to

kick Peppy off. Now the board seemed to have a mind of its own. It took off on a roller coaster ride through the tunnel. The skateboard gained speed, travelling faster and faster. Benny could see Figaro standing alone where they had left him. But there seemed to be no way to stop the speeding wheels. Peppy's eyes were wide with terror. He sat up and grabbed Benny. For a few moments, Peppy tottered out of control.

He clutched at Benny until Benny thought they would both be killed. Finally Peppy let go. In one last try to stand up, he fell off the skateboard. The last Benny saw of his friend before he approached the dangerous hairpin turn ahead, Peppy was sitting on the floor rubbing his bruises.

The skateboard coasted for the corner turn. It was gaining speed. Placing his right foot behind his left, Benny pressed his heel down hard and slightly bent his knees. He regained his balance.

The wall loomed right in front of him. Just in the nick of time, he eased up on his right foot. The board wheeled around at a ninety degree angle. The wall was so close, Benny felt it graze his nose as he steered around the hairpin turn. Then he was out in the open tunnel again on the straightaway.

It was just like the motorcycles Benny had seen at the Forum one night. The drivers had worn crash helmets and goggles. They had leapt through tunnels of fire.

This was a most exciting experience, Benny had to admit. For a few moments, he forgot everything else. The Rink Rats and the Cheddar Cup seemed far away.

Benny was coming to another corner. This one looked more dangerous than the last. The Rink Rats lived just on the other side. Benny braked the board and jumped off. It came to a sudden stop just short of the corner.

Peppy and Figaro came running up behind him.

"Are you all right, captain?" asked Peppy. "We thought you were a goner back there."

"Bravo! A magnificent feat," Figaro said with admiration. "Now on to the final performance. The quest for the Cheddar Cup!"

"Quiet!" Benny said suddenly. The hair rose on the back of his neck.

A low murmur of voices was coming from just beyond the bend.

"I guess it's time we were getting upstairs, gang," Big Boris was saying. "We don't want our little mouse friends to get first choice of food, do we? They're too big for their hockey britches now."

He gave an ugly laugh. The others echoed him with weak imitation laughs.

"I sure am hungry, Boss," said Old Scarface. Benny would recognize Scarface's voice anywhere.

"What about the guardians?" asked one of the Rats.

"We'll bring something back for them," said Big Boris. "They like takeout food. Besides, there should be plenty to eat right here in the dressing room by the end of the game. Come on."

Benny's heart almost stopped beating. What if the Rink Rats came their way? It was dark in the passage, but not dark enough to hide the skateboard. Figaro sat on his haunches, not moving a muscle. Peppy curled up into a ball and froze. None of them dared breathe. The Rink Rats came out into the passage ahead.

"Come on, Boss," said Old Scarface. "Let's take the shortcut. This way."

Old Scarface loomed in front of Benny. But he didn't see him. His back was turned to speak to Boris. Benny couldn't have moved if his life depended upon it.

"Naw," ordered Big Boris. "If we take the other passage, we'll pass the litter bins. There's more food on the floor there. Just the right place to find an appetizer."

Benny was getting hungry just listening to them. He hadn't eaten much that day. He had been too busy.

Abruptly the rats set off in the other direction. Benny didn't change his position for a long time. When all appeared safe, he gave the signal to continue.

Only one thing stood between the mice and the Cheddar Cup now, thought Benny. A couple of scrawny guard rats. Nevertheless, he trembled.

"Benny," Peppy whispered right in his ear, making him jump. "I'm afraid."

Benny pulled himself together and up to his full height. After all, he was the captain. He couldn't fail the team now.

"The bigger they are, the harder they fall," he said firmly. "Forward, team."

# Chapter Six

# A CLOSE SHAVE

A few moments later, Benny approached the Rink Rats' dressing room. His teammates were pressed close behind him. They crawled through the rat hole to the inside.

"What are we doing in here?" Peppy asked. He was shaking from head to tail.

"I have to find something," said Benny. "It's important."

"Most upsetting," said Figaro, glancing around. He looked as if he expected the Rink Rats to jump out any time. "I have a feeling that we are being watched."

"We are alone," Benny assured him. "The guards are too afraid of Big Boris to leave their posts now."

He peered around the room until he saw what he had come for. He hurried over to look at the loudspeaker that lay on the floor.

"We need this for sound effects," he said. "Help me move it closer to the rat hole."

Amongst the three of them, they managed to roll the loudspeaker across the floor to the rat hole and through to the other side. Peppy's nose began to twitch and sniff, and Figaro's ears stood up straight.

"I smell cheese," said Peppy.

"The Cheddar Cup," Benny whispered. "It's right on the other side of that door. The secret room, remember?"

They padded softly across the broken floorboards to the entrance of the secret room. Pressing their noses through the opening, they looked inside.

One of the guards was sound asleep against the wall, snoring loudly. The other sat beside the Cheddar Cup with his chin in his paws. He had a mean and hungry look.

Suddenly he stood up and kicked the other rat.

"Wake up, Packer!" he ordered.

"What's the matter, Sergeant?" The scrawny old rat blinked his eyes. He stood at attention. "Intruders?"

He picked up a board and swung it back and forth.

"Don't be stupid," said Sergeant. "It's not fair. You fall asleep while I stay

awake just to guard this chunk of cheese.
I have better things to do with my time."

"Like what?" asked Packer.

"Like sleep," said Sergeant with
another swift kick. "Why don't I sleep
and you guard the Cup for a change?
We've been holed up here for two days
and nothing has happened yet. And nothing *is* going to happen. We've seen the
last of those mice. In the meantime, Big
Boris and the others are eating good garbage. We just sit here and starve to
death."

Benny's ears burned and his nose
twitched with anger. He'd show those
rats! He crawled inside the loudspeaker
and took a deep breath. Then he yelled as
loudly as possible. He tried to make his
voice sound like Big Boris's.

"Attention, guards!" he cried. "Hard
times are here."

The loud noise echoed through the
tunnel.

The two rats jumped to their feet and
saluted. Benny smothered a giggle. It
looked as if the plan were going to work.
The two rats really thought he was Big
Boris!

"Take the Cheddar Cup out through

the back door," Benny ordered. He felt braver by the minute. "Load the Cup onto the skateboard. Then come to the garbage cans on the north side of the Forum. We'll have to store as much food as we can because there are bad days ahead."

Benny held his breath. Had the guards recognized his voice?

"Hard times are here," screamed Packer. "Did you hear that, Sergeant? Why don't we eat the Cup ourselves and make our getaway?"

"I'm in charge here!" Sergeant shouted. "We will obey Big Boris, our leader. Get moving!"

Benny's heart thudded. Peppy and Figaro stood close behind him as he watched the rats struggle with the Cheddar Cup. They pushed it to the opening in the baseboards. They tipped the Cup over on its side. For a moment it looked as if the Cup would break into a million pieces. Then the two rats safely pushed it through the opening into the tunnel.

"They fell for it!" Benny whispered. "Hook, line, and sinker."

"I hope so, captain," said Figaro. "It seems almost too good to be true."

"Good planning," Benny said modestly. He stepped back inside the megaphone and bellowed again. "Guards! Have you put the Cup on the wheels?"

"Yeah, Boss!" called Sergeant. "Can we go and get some grub now?"

"Guards dismissed!" Benny yelled. His voice cracked on the last note, but the rats were too excited to pay attention. Benny and his teammates hid inside the loudspeaker. Peppy trembled, but Figaro sat quietly. The rats charged out of the passage, through the secret room. Then they raced into the locker room.

Benny felt the megaphone rock as the guard rats ran past. When all was silent, Benny crawled out with the others. They danced around in a circle.

"You did it, captain," said Peppy. "You tricked them."

"There's no time to waste," Figaro said suddenly. He stopped dancing. "There's no telling how soon Big Boris will discover the theft."

"You're right, Figaro," Benny said. "We don't have much time to get the Cup home."

They rushed through the empty dressing room. The crowds shouted and stamped overhead. Someone had scored a goal in the playoff game. Now the mice were out in the tunnel. There was the Cheddar Cup perched safely on the skateboard. It was theirs now, thought Benny proudly. He scarcely had a moment to stop and admire it. He would look at the Cup later when it was home once again.

He gave the skateboard a push and it began to roll slowly. The Cup gave it just enough steadiness to stay on course. Once Benny had made the first turn, he relaxed. Then he heard a sound that turned his blood cold. The Rink Rats were coming back!

"What do you mean, *I* ordered you to take the Cheddar Cup?" Big Boris screamed. "I've been over at the snack bar all night."

"But Boss," cried Packer, "we heard you give the orders. You said hard times were here."

"Rubbish!" Big Boris cried. "Times have never been better. There's more food in the Forum than our ancestors ever dreamed of. I smell a mouse. A seedy little bullet-sized mouse who wants the Cheddar Cup back. He'll stop at nothing to get it."

"The mice can't have gone far, Boss," said Sergeant. "We can still catch them."

"You'd better catch them," said Big Boris. "Fast."

Benny listened in horror to the noise from the Rink Rats' locker room. The Rats scuffled about and bumped into each other. Their heavy breathing could be heard in the corridor. They rushed into the tunnel. "I have to do something to save the Cup," Benny told himself wildly. A plan began to form in his mind.

"Stay close to the Cheddar Cup, team," he told Peppy and Figaro. "Don't abandon it, no matter what."

"What about you, captain?" asked Peppy. "You're not going to abandon us, are you?"

"I'll stay behind, Peppy," Benny said. "When the Rink Rats find me alone, they'll chase me instead of you and the Cup. Hurry! There's no time to argue."

Reluctantly Peppy and Figaro pushed the skateboard around the next turn. When they were out of sight, Benny shoved back his shoulders. The Rink Rats were so close, he could feel their hot breath on his neck.

"There he is!" cried Big Boris. "After

him! He's got the Cheddar Cup."

Benny took a deep breath and then plunged into the corridor. He took a right turn instead of a left. Above, he heard the roar that signalled the end of the hockey game. Thousands of human feet thundered down the stairs. The organ music swelled to fill the Forum with sound.

Benny ran as fast as his feet would carry him. He ran through dark tunnels and around dangerous turns. The Rink Rats were right behind him. Up ahead he spotted a brightly lit opening.

Big Boris almost caught Benny's tail, but Benny managed to outdistance the rat. He headed for the light ahead. It was a mouse-sized opening. Benny ran for his life. He reached the hole and slipped through to the other side.

What was happening? His feet flew out from under him and he skimmed across the slippery surface of the ice. He found himself flat on his back looking up at the enormous electric clock and scoreboard high in the rafters of the Forum. He scrambled to his feet, but he was on the ice without skates, slipping and sliding. The bright lights from overhead blinded him.

Benny skidded along towards a big machine. The man at the wheel didn't notice Benny. He whistled and fixed his eyes on the ice straight ahead.

Cleaning the ice and spraying boiling water on the surface, the machine was a hundred times more dreadful than any cleaning equipment Benny had ever seen.

And he was headed straight for this grinding churning monster!

## Chapter Seven

# THE GREAT ZAMBONI MACHINE

BENNY panicked. The Zamboni machine came towards him. It had rubber tires and sparkling mag wheels. They rolled closer and closer. Benny scrambled to his feet, but then fell again. It was hard to stand up on the ice without skates. The Zamboni was within a whisker, when it suddenly churned away into the end zone.

Benny didn't know what to do now. He looked back at the boards to the mousehole he had just left. Two Rink Rats leered out at him. He couldn't go back the same way he had come in.

His best chance was to head for the other side of the rink and try to escape through the open boards. Carefully he placed one foot in front of the other to keep from falling.

The big machine continued to clear the

ice. The horizontal auger shaved a few centimetres from the top while the hot pipe released a cascade of boiling water over the newly scraped surface. The felt pad in the rear smoothed it to a mirror shine.

Benny managed to stay on his feet for a couple of seconds until he reached the freshly iced path of the Zamboni. He could see his own reflection. A second later he went sprawling.

Benny slid across the wide ice path. How he wished for a pair of skates! But there was no time for wishing. The machine was heading for Benny again. He couldn't make it to the far side of the rink and safety.

He had to think fast.

Then Benny knew. There was only one chance. If he jumped up on the Zamboni on the next pass, he could make it to the only safe place on the back of the machine—the steel guard covering the auger. But if he became caught between the wheels, the boiling water would scald him to death and the felt pad would scrape up his remains.

Benny waited for the Zamboni to pass. At the last possible moment, he leapt into the air. He made it to the steel guard on his first jump, and clung to the edge. With a great effort, he pulled himself up on the guard and huddled in the corner.

Above, Benny saw the seat where the driver sat, but the man didn't notice him. The horrid sharp-pointed steel blades continued their work. Benny began to choke and gasp from the machine's exhaust fumes. He covered his face to keep the fumes from making him sick. The whirring noise of the Zamboni struck terror in his heart. He wondered if he would ever get out of this alive.

The Zamboni made two more trips over the rink and then headed for the gate on the far side of the Forum.

Benny had never felt so hot. The sweat ran down his face, blinding his eyes. He could hardly breathe. It was like a steam bath, Benny thought. "That's it for tonight, Jake," said the driver to the man who swung open the gate.

"Drop the ice in here," said Jake as the Zamboni swung out through the wide exit. The blades and pad lifted.

Below him, Benny saw a shallow pit filled with ice shavings. The driver dumped the load of ice into the pit. The man called Jake swept the loose chunks of ice onto a shovel and into the wheel-barrow.

It was now or never, Benny decided. He had to make a break for it.

He braced himself on the edge of the steel guard. The wheelbarrow seemed closer and less menacing then the pit where the scraped shavings were piled. He took a deep breath and jumped.

Benny landed with a shock in the wheelbarrow on a blanket of ice. The sweat froze on his body. His teeth chattered and he shivered violently.

Jake now had another shovelfull of ice shavings. For a moment, Benny wondered if he should have stayed with the Zamboni and taken his chances. The shovelfull of ice was aimed straight at him. It hit all at once, leaving Benny breathless and shaking.

Gamely he fought his way through the snowy heap to the top and looked out.

The man with the broom and shovel stared down at him.

## Chapter Eight

# THE GARBAGE TRUCK

TRAPPED in the wheelbarrow with the ice, Benny looked up at the ugly face staring down at him. It was even uglier than that of Big Boris. The face belonged to a man with a bald head, bulging eyes streaked with red veins, and a stubble of black beard.

"What have we here?" asked Jake. "A mouse! Must have scooped him up in my shovel. Tough little fellow, aren't you?"

Benny's heart pounded in his chest. He couldn't have moved if his life depended upon it—which it did. The man reached a hairy hand into the opening, picked Benny up by the tail, and dangled him in the air.

"Well, we can't have mice in the Forum," Jake said aloud. "I'll just throw you in the garbage."

The man walked outside and tossed

Benny into a big container beside the door. Benny landed in a heap of junk—papers, boxes, hot dogs, and spoiled fruits and vegetables. The man dusted off his hands and wiped them on his pants.

"Happy landing!" he shouted with a coarse laugh.

Benny stood up in a mountain of garbage. He thought about his situation. Things could be worse, he decided. He had survived the harrowing ordeal on the Zamboni, only to be dumped into a garbage bin. Besides his dignity, nothing was hurt. And he *had* escaped from the Rink Rats. Now all he had to do was crawl out and hurry back to the Forum. His team would be lost without him, he knew.

Although Benny was surrounded by more food than he had ever seen before, he didn't feel the least bit hungry. His only concern was for the Cheddar Cup. He hoped that Peppy and Figaro had wheeled it home to their locker room before the Rink Rats found it.

Benny smiled as he thought of the merry chase through the tunnels. He was sure the Cup must be safe by now.

From St. Catherine Street, Benny heard a loud clanking noise. The Zamboni again? Should he lie low and wait for the noise to go away? Perhaps he should make a run for it before it was too late. He scrambled along the edge of the container to the top and looked out.

A truck pulled to a stop beside him. Benny saw number fifty-one painted on its side.

"You've got a passenger, Sam," the man with the bald head yelled from the doorway. "I just threw a mouse into the garbage."

"Well, he'll find lots of company down at the dump." The driver laughed. "This is my last stop tonight. See you a bit earlier tomorrow night, Jake. Maybe you can get me in to watch the last period."

"No problem," said Jake. "Come in through the back door, Sam."

He waved. The driver shoved a lever. The back end of the truck clanged and rattled as the hydraulic lift lowered towards the container. Benny felt himself being lifted into the air along with the garbage and dumped into the back of the truck. He landed with a heavy thud. Garbage of all kinds showered down on Benny. An apple core and two paper cups struck him on the head. When he opened his mouth, he swallowed wet coffee grounds.

The papers, boxes, and rotting food continued to cover Benny until he was buried beneath the trash. He thought he would suffocate if he didn't get air. At last the rattling and clanging noises stopped. The driver shifted into gear and, with a lurch, the truck pulled away from the Forum.

Benny fought his way to the top of the heap. He watched his home disappear down the street. It was splendid, he thought proudly. No wonder so many people came to such a beautiful building. The Forum had been his home, the only home he had ever known.

Benny wiped a tear from his eye as he jolted and bounced along the street on the back of number fifty-one dump truck.

The city was very bright, Benny thought. In the distance he saw the lights from Mount Royal sparkling in the night sky. A cross glittered on top of the Mount. Lights shone everywhere. Buildings glowed, and neon signs blinked on and off. But nowhere were the lights as bright as at the Forum when the NHL teams took to the ice in a hockey game. As the truck picked up speed at the outskirts of the city, Benny wondered if he would ever see his beloved home again.

The truck sped along an old dirt road. It was a rough ride. Benny had to concentrate all his attention on keeping his bones and ribs from being broken. Down a steep hill they went. Finally the truck jolted to a stop.

It was quiet for a moment. Benny wondered what would happen next. The clanking and creaking began again. Slowly the back end of the truck lifted higher and higher into the air. Benny clung wildly to an iron ring, but lost his grip. He tumbled down, down, down into the open pit of garbage that yawned below.

Benny sat in the darkness. He listened to the whining and screeching of the truck as the last bit of garbage fell. At last the truck pulled away.

Benny rummaged through the trash and made his way out to fresh air. He found the rough road the truck had used. Slowly he crawled along in the track of the fresh tire marks. Every bone in his body ached.

Overhead, the full moon shone in the

sky. Thousands of stars twinkled. Benny had never seen anything quite like it. But the sky only reminded him of the many lights outside the Forum.

Benny felt absolutely and utterly alone—more alone than he had ever felt in his life. He wondered what Figaro and Peppy were doing now. He would give anything to be home with them.

He yawned sleepily and closed his eyes. It had been a long hard night. At last Benny fell into a fitful sleep.

## Chapter Nine

# THE BIG M

BENNY awoke in the morning to the sun burning down on his back. It was a new feeling. He had lived all his life inside the Forum. When he opened his eyes, it was hard to see under such a bright blue sky. Benny squinted and then scampered under an old broken armchair where it was cool. He peered out at his new home. Mounds and mounds of garbage stretched as far as the eye could see. The food wasn't choice, as it had been in the Forum. But still, it was food. Benny rummaged around until he found a soggy half-eaten soda cracker. He ate his breakfast. It was a fine morning, and it felt good to be alive.

The garbage dump seemed deserted. Benny decided to go looking for other mice.

He saw a small shack in the distance, with smoke curling out of the chimney. Benny ventured closer. He noticed a small patch of ice on the ground near the shack. Something was moving around on the ice. Benny's curiosity was aroused. He ran along the edge of the path. He stopped, twitching his whiskers.

On the ice was another mouse! It was a big grey mouse sporting a red, white, and blue sweater with the letter M on the front. Wire-rimmed spectacles sat on the mouse's nose. The mouse was knocking a bit of rubber eraser around on the ice with a twig.

"He shoots, he scores!" cried the other mouse as he sent the rubber to the far side of the frozen puddle, between two tin can markers. An old minnow net strung between the markers caught the puck.

Benny approached the big mouse.

"What are you playing?" asked Benny. "Looks a lot like hockey. But it isn't *real* hockey."

"Maybe it is, and maybe it isn't." Leaning on his stick, the other mouse turned to look at Benny. "It's called street hockey around here."

"Where's the rest of your team?"

"I am the team."

"That can't be much fun." Benny sounded sympathetic.

"It's better than no hockey at all." He shrugged. "The others down here don't go in much for sports. I'm different. I love hockey. I watch every game on the TV set in the watchman's shed." He nodded at the little shack with the smoke curling out of the chimney.

"Where I come from," Benny confided, "we play every night all year round. Even in the summer we have ice."

"Sounds like the Great Beyond," said the other mouse. "The ice will soon melt here. Spring is coming."

"There's nothing strange about having ice all year round, you know," Benny told him. "A giant machine at the Forum keeps the ice hard and smooth even in the summer. It's called a Zamboni. That's why I'm here. I was scooped up in it."

He told the other mouse his story. "I've got to get back to the Forum in time for the big Cheddar Cup playoffs," Benny finished.

At his words, the big mouse grabbed Benny's arm tightly. His whiskers twitched. "Did I hear right?" He peered at Benny through wire-rimmed spectacles. "You did say the Cheddar Cup, didn't you?"

"I certainly did. It's just about the most important thing in my life. And to think I'm going to miss it after all my hopes and plans!"

He began to feel sorry for himself, but the big mouse was dancing around in circles.

"Then it's not just a legend after all," he cried happily. He kicked one of the tin can markers and sent it spinning across the ice. "It's true. Every single word my grandfather told me is true."

"You've heard of the Cheddar Cup?" Benny sounded surprised. "I had no idea it was so famous."

"Its fame has spread," said the big mouse. "My grandfather played hockey in the old MHL. They called him the Big M. That's short for the Big Mouse. I'm named after him. Grandfather talked about nothing else but hockey until the day he left for the Great Beyond."

Benny walked around the big mouse and looked him over.

"What position do you play?" he asked.

"I'm not sure," said the Big M. "I think defence. Yes, I'm sure I would play good defence."

"We need defencemen," Benny told

him. "But what about those glasses? Hockey players don't usually wear glasses."

"No problem," said the Big M. He took the wire-rimmed spectacles off and blew through the empty frames. He tucked them into his pocket. "There's no glass in them. I can see perfectly well without them."

"Why do you wear them?"

"They make me look more intelligent, of course."

"Of course," Benny agreed. "There's nothing wrong in that, I suppose."

He buried his chin in his paws and gazed out over the garbage dump. Wisps of black smoke curled into the air from smoking fires.

"They're burning your food," Benny said.

"Not to worry," said the Big M. "They bring in fresh food every day. Actually, we have quite a fine diet here. If you stay, will you teach me how to play *real* hockey?"

Benny ignored the question. He didn't want to be rude, but he also didn't want to live in the garbage dump forever. He tried to think.

"This is my first trip out," he said carefully. "It's not what I expected it to be at all."

"Things are never what you expect them to be," agreed the Big M.

"I want to go home!" said Benny, momentarily forgetting his good manners. "I miss the Forum."

"You don't want to stay here?" asked the Big M, astonished. "There's more than enough food."

"I know," said Benny, "and I'm not knocking it. But the food here has been picked over already. It's second best. At the Forum we eat the best food money can buy."

Both mice were silent for a moment.

"The Forum is my home," said Benny. "It's the only real home I've ever known. I've got to get back in time for the Cheddar Cup."

"If only I could see a real mouse team play for the Cheddar Cup just once before I go to the Great Beyond!" sighed the Big M. "Then I could die happy."

"You'll do better than just seeing them," Benny assured him. He stood up suddenly and shook the Big M's paw. "You can be on my team. You can play defence."

The Big M was speechless for a moment.

"You won't be sorry," he vowed. "I won't let anyone past me. I've watched the pros play on television. I know all the moves."

"Now, if only we could think of a way to get back to the Forum," said Benny.

"I'm not sure how to get out of the dump," said the Big M. "I've never been out before."

He put on his wire spectacles and paced up and down on a charred stump of wood. He folded his hands behind his back.

"Do you need your glasses to see now?" asked Benny.

"No," the Big M told him, "but they definitely help me to think better, of course."

"Of course," agreed Benny.

The Big M stopped pacing. "I think there's only one way to get out," he said finally.   "How's that?"

"The same way you came in, Benny." He removed his glasses and tucked them inside his sweater. His voice lowered. "In the garbage truck. We'll both ride out of here first class on number fifty-one dump truck. Each truck takes the same route at about the same time every day. I've heard the drivers talking to the watchman."

"You're right," cried Benny. "I heard the driver of number fifty-one say he was going back to the Forum tonight. He wants to see the end of the big game."

"That's perfect," said the Big M.

"It's our only hope," said Benny. "But first, we'll wait until dark."

# Chapter Ten

# THE DUMP

THE dump slowly came to life. The old watchman who lived in the shack came outside, scratched himself, squinted at the sun, and then went back into the shed. Early morning garbage trucks shunted into the yard to dump fresh rubbish over the old. A covey of starlings screamed and fought with one another for food. Everywhere, piles of old garbage burned to heaps of black rubble.

Benny was glad that the big grey mouse was going with him. The team needed all the help it could get. Especially if it ever came to a showdown for the Cheddar Cup between the Mice and the Rink Rats. The Big M looked like a good player—a natural.

"There's less chance of being seen at night," said the Big M. "We'll hitch a ride on number fifty-one on the last run."

"In the meantime," said Benny, "we'd

better catch some sleep. We'll need to be wide awake tonight. Besides, I didn't sleep well yesterday. Not well at all."

The Big M nodded sympathetically.

The two of them scurried up and down hills and around mounds of rubble until they reached an old car.

"Well, here it is," said the Big M proudly. "This is where I sleep during the day."

He had fixed up his place quite nicely, Benny thought. The seats were soft and comfortable, with big wads of kapok stuffing bursting from them.

"I like to sit by the fire before retiring for the day," said the Big M. He seated himself by the garbage fire near the car, stretching out his paws to warm them. Benny sat beside him.

"Are you sure there aren't any others who want to play hockey down here?" he asked.

"No," said the Big M sadly. He poked at the fire with a twig. "They play hide and seek with the rats, and chase each other around all night long. They aren't the least bit interested in hockey. They've never even seen a game on television. They think I'm a little strange up here."

He tapped his forehead.

"Well, I don't think you're the least bit strange," said Benny indignantly. He picked up a stick and poked at the fire, too. It felt warm and comfortable. "Anyone who doesn't play hockey is strange if you ask me."

"They think I'm not a good mixer," confided the Big M. "But it's not true. They want me to do the things *they* want me to do. They don't understand why I'm different. So they mostly leave me alone."

"At the Forum you'll fit in just fine," Benny told him. "Almost everyone plays hockey all night long there."

"I live a good life here," said the Big M. "Plenty of food. Hockey on television every Wednesday and Saturday night in the watchman's shed. Lots of frozen puddles to practise on in the winter. I've never complained. It's been a good life. At least it was until you arrived and told me about the Cheddar Cup. You've made me want to go and see it."

"You're needed at the Forum," Benny told him. "Wait until the other mice see you. Lucky I found you."

"I think it was Fate," said the Big M.

He yawned sleepily and stood up. "Well, time for a nap. We'll be safe inside the car."

They ran through a small rusted hole in the door and curled up on the soft stuffing to wait—and sleep if possible—until nightfall.

Benny had terrible dreams of his wild ride to the dump, and of almost being smothered to death in rotting garbage. He hoped the ride home would be more comfortable and that he would live to tell the tale. He had to get back to the Forum safe and sound. It was important.

As Benny fell asleep, he thought about Peppy and Figaro. They would be curled up in the locker room in their favourite beds—hockey pads and gloves. He wondered if they missed him as much as he missed them. They were probably glad to be rid of him. Without him, they wouldn't have any bossy captain giving them orders.

Benny didn't know how long he had slept when he awoke suddenly.

There was a hot prickly feeling on his neck—the strange sensation of being watched. Benny opened his eyes and blinked. It was almost dark. The sun going down over the dump mottled the sky like marbled cheese.

Benny had no time to admire the sunset. The fiery green eyes of a mangy striped cat glared at him in the twilight.

A low throaty noise came from the cat. It sent spikes of fear up Benny's spine. His heart thumped wildly. "Danger!" he cried.

The Big M awoke with a start. "What is it? Is it time?"

Benny tried to speak, but couldn't find his voice. At the sound of the Big M's voice, the cat had become even more excited. Benny saw the tip of its tail swishing faster and faster. The cat crouched on the hood ready for the kill. Then Benny noticed that the cracked glass of the windshield covered almost the entire window.

"Don't move!" ordered the Big M. "The cat can't get in through the windshield. And the other windows are rolled up. We're perfectly safe here."

Safe, thought Benny wildly. If this was safe, then he wanted no part of it. The quicker they got out of this garbage dump, the better.

## Chapter Eleven

# THE CAT

THE cat placed a paw on the cracked windshield and quickly drew it back. Then it settled back on its haunches to wait. Cats could be the most patient creatures in the world, Benny knew. Once, a cat had trapped his aunt for two days in a storage bin. His aunt had barely escaped. Benny's heart beat more calmly now. The Big M was right. The cat couldn't get inside. But it *was* unnerving having the great striped creature sit right outside on the hood of the car. Benny hated feeling trapped.

It was a war of nerves.

The sky grew darker and darker. The stars and a full moon came out again. The cat shifted slightly and placed its head between its paws. It pretended to close its green eyes, but Benny knew better. Every few seconds, he could see glowing slits as the cat opened its eyes again to see if he and the Big M had moved.

"I'm not going to sit here a minute longer," Benny announced suddenly. "I'm going to make a break for it."

"A break for what?" asked the Big M. "The Great Beyond?"

"Freedom!" cried Benny.

The more he thought about it, the better he liked the idea. Each time another garbage truck came lumbering down the dirt track, he was afraid it might be number fifty-one with the last load of the night. What if they missed their ride back to the Forum?

"Better to be a live prisoner here than a dead hockey player," remarked the Big M.

"I'm going to chance it anyway," said Benny. "Are you coming with me? Do you want to play for the Cheddar Cup or rot in this dump forever?"

Outside on the hood, the cat twitched its tail back and forth, back and forth. Both eyes were wide open now.

"Well, if you put it that way," said the Big M, "it's the Cheddar Cup for me."

"Good," said Benny. "Follow me!"

Benny crept down to the car's rotting floorboards. The Big M followed. The cat grew more excited. It paced back and forth across the hood. The sound from its throat seemed louder than the Zamboni machine.

"We'll escape through the floor-boards," Benny whispered "By the time the cat has found out what happened, we'll be long gone."

"To the Great Beyond," muttered the Big M gloomily.

"Nonsense!" said Benny. Nevertheless, his heart pounded.

He scurried through the hole in the floorboards with the Big M close behind him. He ran along the muffler to the edge of the tailpipe. The cat was nowhere in sight. Was it still on the hood? They waited for what seemed hours, although really only seconds had ticked by.

The moonlight streamed down on the endless hills and hollows of the dump. Bright moonlight washed the landscape. A few clouds scudded across the sky. Benny decided to wait until the clouds hid the moon.

In the distance, Benny heard the rattling and clanging of a garbage truck rolling down the road.

"That's it!" cried the Big M. "It's number fifty-one. I can tell."

"The last trip of the night?" asked Benny.

The Big M nodded tensely.

"Get ready to make a run for it," Benny whispered. "As soon as the clouds hide the moon."

"It's no use," said the Big M. "Cats can see very well in the dark."

The two mice waited and waited on the car's tailpipe as the moonlight continued to bask the dump in silver. The truck rumbled closer and closer. It was travelling faster than it had the night before.

"In a minute," whispered the Big M nervously, "it will be too late."

The truck jolted to a stop, the hydraulic lift cranking into position. Fresh garbage tumbled to the ground.

"Now!" Benny ordered.

He scrambled along the car's tailpipe, and across the frame to the inside of the tires. At last he felt firm ground beneath him. The Big M was right behind. At the same instant, the cat gave a blood-curdling meow and sprang down.

Benny and the Big M raced across the open land. A cloud partly hid the moon. Benny ran until he felt his chest would burst. The Big M caught up with him, and they ran side by side. Benny felt a sharp pain as the cat pounced on his tail. He was jolted to a stop.

"Get to the truck, Big M!" yelled Benny.

The cat released Benny's tail, and then crouched in front of him. A striped paw reached out towards Benny. One of the claws drew blood from his flank. He curled up in a tight little ball.

Another swipe of the cat's paw caught Benny at the shoulder. It drew more blood, and the pain made him wince.

Suddenly an idea came to him. He could pretend that the cat was in front of an open hockey net. The cat could be the only player between Benny and a goal. In the matter of goals, Benny used instinct. Body and mind worked together perfectly as he fooled his opponent.

"Hurry up, Benny!" the Big M called from the garbage truck. "Make a run for it!"

Benny planned his escape. As he moved slightly, the cat was content to sit and watch him. Its green eyes glowed in the dark. Pretending he had a hockey puck cradled against his stick and that he was skating through the defence for the net, Benny suddenly ran to the left, straight for the cat.

The cat was startled. No mouse had ever charged it before. It acted on instinct. It crouched and sprang. In that split second, Benny veered sharply to the right, as if he were headed for the net. He saw ahead of him a clear opening. He had deked the cat out of position.

The moon burst through the clouds and Benny saw the hydraulic lift of the truck grind back into position.

Joyfully, Benny raced across the open field, up and down hills and hollows towards the garbage truck. The cat ran close behind. But Benny no longer cared. He had gained the precious time he needed.

"The truck's leaving!" screamed the Big M.

Benny could see him now, perched on the large red tail-light.

The truck driver lurched into low gear and began the slow crawl up the hill. Benny cut across the track, blood pounding in his ears. At the last possible moment, the Big M reached down from the tail-light. Benny grabbed both of his front paws just as the cat sprang at the truck. Too late! The truck gathered speed. The cat yowled in anger on the dirt road...disappointed to have missed a tasty meal.

"You made it! You made it!" cried the Big M, clapping Benny on the shoulder.

## Chapter Twelve

# THE HERO RETURNS

BENNY and the Big M rested happily against the bumper. As the truck left the dump behind, Benny looked at the moonlit landscape for what he hoped was the last time.

"I've seen enough of the Great Outdoors," he confided.

"So have I, for now," The Big M agreed. "Now it's on to the Cheddar Cup and victory!"

"We'll soon be home," murmured Benny in utter contentment.

The truck joggled comfortably through brightly lit streets. Neon signs blinked on and off. Lighted displays glowed inside store windows. Then, up ahead, Benny saw the lights of the Forum.

"That's it!" Benny cried, grabbing the Big M and shaking him. "That's the Forum. We're home."

The truck jolted to a stop beside the familiar waste disposal bin at the back door.

"Come on!" cried Benny. "Let's get out of here before we end up back in the garbage bin."

They scrambled down the side of the truck to the street below, through the open door, and into the Forum.

For a moment, Benny was overcome with emotion. Everything looked exactly as it always had. The crowds shouted and cheered. The Canadiens whizzed across the ice, blades flashing, sticks crashing, bodies bruising.

With deep satisfaction, Benny breathed in the familiar air. It was charged with excitement. There was no place on earth quite like home, he thought. He couldn't wait to introduce his new friend to Peppy and Figaro. The Big M followed him through the corridors and tunnels that ran between the spaces in the walls.

At last they reached the Home Team locker room. It was empty.

"Funny," Benny mused. "Well, maybe the other mice are watching the game. That's where we get the best food. Up in the stands."

The big mouse nodded. He closed his eyes and sniffed the air.

"It smells like hockey," he said. He opened his eyes and looked around the room. He saw the sweaters, sticks, gloves, shin pads, and old sneakers.

"Comfortable," he said slowly. "Very comfortable. It beats the watchman's shed. Although I did enjoy his hot stove."

"We have a hot stove league here, too," Benny said eagerly. "It's upstairs near the broadcasting booth. The players and experts sit around after the games. They talk about what the teams did wrong, who was to blame for all the bad plays, the referee, and stuff like that. We don't go upstairs very often."

The Big M nodded. "I suppose there's no need for it," he said. "You have every-thing you need right here."

Benny cleared his throat. Maybe it was time to tell the Big M a little more about the Rink Rats.

"Here's our Waiting Room." Benny zipped in through the knothole in the floorboards. "We spend a lot of time in here waiting. We have to wait for the Canadiens to leave every night. Some-times they take forever."

Peppy and Figaro weren't in the Waiting Room. Benny led the way to the tunnel by the other floorboard hole.

"How do you know where you're going?" asked the Big M.

"You'll get used to it," said Benny. "We have the run of the place. Except for the Visiting Team's dressing room. That's where the Rink Rats hang out. You'll have to steer clear of them. Mostly, they stick to their business and we stick to ours. Except now, their business *is* our business. They stole the Cheddar Cup from us."

"Stole the Cheddar Cup!"

Benny nodded.

"In my grandfather's time. But we managed to get it out of the Rink Rats' secret room the night of my adventure. Peppy and Figaro were in charge of rolling the Cup back to our side of the Forum. I tried to sidetrack the Rink Rats by running in the opposite direction."

"What happened then?"

"I'm not sure," said Benny, rubbing his chin thoughtfully. "We had the Cup in the outer tunnel. The heist was going just as planned. Then I ended up taking a wrong turn and landed out on the ice.

That's when I tangled with the Zamboni. You know the rest."

The Big M nodded.

"Peppy and Figaro might have had time to roll the Cup back when the rats were chasing me," said Benny. "By now, reinforcements should have arrived. We advertised for mouse hockey players for the championship Cheddar Cup game."

Benny and the Big M had entered the long tunnel beyond the Waiting Room. In the distance, they heard the low murmur of voices. There was a crack of light beneath the floorboards.

"Follow me!" ordered Benny the Bullet.

They entered the room by a large knothole. Then Benny sat perfectly still. He stared at the strange scene before him. His heart beat faster. The Cheddar Cup sat in the middle of the tunnel. Peppy and Figaro had managed to roll it back home.

Peppy la Pierre, Figaro the Flyer, Anne Marie, and several other mice stood beside Benny's hockey stick. It had been propped up in a crack in the floor. Benny's red, blue, and white number nine sweater was draped over the marker.

Figaro spoke in his most eloquent voice.

"I shall now read the inscription to our beloved and dearly departed friend, Benny the Bullet:
In Loving Memory
Here lies the spirit of Benny the Bullet
Our Captain
Who Disappeared in the Great Zamboni Machine.
He was a great hockey player and a good true friend."

Anne Marie wrote rapidly in her notebook. Peppy la Pierre sniffled loudly and Raphaela held a handkerchief to her eyes. This jolted Benny to his senses.

"Hold it!" Benny shouted, running over to the marker. "What's going on here?"

Peppy and Figaro were stunned. Raphaela stopped crying. Anne Marie crumpled the notepaper she had been writing on, but not before Benny read the headline.

MICE MOURN UNTIMELY DEATH OF BENNY THE BULLET.

"You're alive!" Figaro said softly. "You're alive!"

"A ghost!" cried Peppy. *"Mon Dieu."* He crossed himself.

"I'm no ghost," cried Benny, stamping his foot. "I'm alive and well, as you can see. What are you doing holding a funeral service for me?"

"It was a beautiful funeral." Peppy wiped tears from his eyes. "You should have been here."

Benny was touched in spite of himself.

"Sorry I missed it. Maybe next time."

"Figaro gave the most beautiful eulogy."

"Actually it was from grand opera," said Figaro modestly. He grabbed Benny and kissed him on both cheeks. "But I meant it, nevertheless. Every single word. Right from the heart."

"It was a work of art," said Raphaela admiringly.

"Stuff and nonsense," Benny said gruffly.

He yanked his sweater off the marker, pulled it on over his head, and then wiped his nose on the sleeve of his sweater.

"Rats," he muttered. "I'm not ready for the Great Beyond yet."

Peppy and Figaro were overcome with emotion.

"Here," Benny said, quickly changing the subject, "meet our new defenceman. The Big M."

"Not related to *the* famous Big M, the hockey player, by any chance?" Peppy asked.

"One and the same," the Big M said proudly, adjusting his spectacles. "And I'm here to help you get back the Cheddar Cup."

Benny looked pleased with his new discovery. "I hope so," he commented. "We certainly need all the help we can get."

## Chapter Thirteen

# THE CHALLENGE

BENNY tacked a sign over the snack bar door.

Sunday Morning—1:00 A.M. Sharp
Championship Cheddar Cup Game
Everyone Welcome
Refreshments: Free
Admission: Free

The next evening, mouse hockey players from the Outside who had heard the news came to try out for the championship team. Benny was happy to see Howie Squeaker, a respected veteran of hockey, among the hopefuls. An added surprise was a Russian import named Malenky. Malenky had come to the country in the duffle bag of a visiting Russian hockey player who had defected during a Team Canada game. The duffle bag had been left on a train in *Le Métro* by the

Russian player. It had been at the Atwater station. Malenky had heard about the championship Cheddar Cup game from a *Métro* mouse. Together they had braved the tunnelwork of Westmount Square to come and fight for the Cheddar Cup at the Forum.

Benny led the mice through the drills. As they skated backwards, Benny noted the best skaters. Then they practised rushes against the goalie. The Big M and Malenky played the best defence. No forwards from the Great Outdoors were better than Figaro, except perhaps Howie Squeaker. Benny put Squeaker, Figaro, and himself down on the first line of one team. He also chose second and third lines and extra defence.

Tension mounted as they practised hour after hour for the big game. So far the Rink Rats hadn't come near the ice.

At last Saturday night arrived.

Benny, Peppy, and Figaro took up their regulation box seats to watch the Canadiens and the Leafs in the last game of the Stanley Cup playoffs. They waved to Raphaela, Mizzy, and Anne Marie, who were peeking out from the broadcast booth. But Benny the Bullet found it hard to concentrate. He was too keyed up for their own game, which was to follow immediately.

The Canadiens won in the final minutes of the game. The three stars skated out on the ice to the tune of "Happy Days Are Here Again." A red carpet rolled out; officials in dark suits made speeches. They presented the winning captain with the silver Stanley Cup.

Back in the crowded Waiting Room after the game, Benny and the others watched the Canadiens fill the silver cup with champagne, drink it down, and pour it over one another's heads.

"You can bet we won't do that with the Cheddar Cup," said Peppy. "We're going to fill it with cheese and eat every bite. We won't waste any."

After what seemed like forever, the Canadiens turned off the lights. They left the dressing room, laughing and joking as they went up the stairs.

"I thought they'd never leave," said Benny. "Come on! Let's get our equipment together."

From out of the secret hiding places in the Waiting Room, they piled all the equipment on the floor. Some of the sweaters matched. There were shin guards made from old hockey programs and ticket stubs—to be worn on the legs with elastic bands.

The Big M, who was clever at turning useless junk into useful gear, had made face guards from an old piece of wire screen. Sticks were an assortment of twigs, popsicle and lollipop sticks, and pencil stubs. All had hard curved blades glued to them, and were taped with plastic adhesive strips.

Peppy, being the goalie, had the best equipment of all. He had gnawed through a spot in a goalie pad and managed to take out just enough deer hair for his own pads. The hole was so small that the Canadien goalie would never even miss the stuffing. Peppy's pads were the best money could buy.

"Look at your socks, Peppy," said Benny, disgusted.

One was orange. The other was red, blue, and white.

"They bring me luck, captain," insisted Peppy. "I couldn't play goal without them."

Howie Squeaker had gnawed a smooth round chunk from a regulation black rubber puck. For the first time, they had a real puck of just the proper size.

The mice were tense, and ready for the game to begin. First, though, they had to wait for the grinding scraping noise of the Zamboni machine to stop.

They all remembered too well the night Benny had disappeared in the Zamboni.

When the machine left the ice, the overhead lights darkened, leaving only the night lights to burn softly. It was time to take to the ice.

The mice started the warm-up...skating around in circles, skating backwards, doing figure eights, slapping their sticks against the ice.

"The ice is fast tonight, team," Benny announced. "It should be a good game. Those finky Rats haven't shown up yet and it doesn't look as if they're going to. So we'll just have to play for the Cup amongst ourselves."

"Good riddance to bad rubbish," said Peppy.

They marked out the playing area with a grease pencil inside the red circle, of the face-off zone. A hairnet and an old sieve served for nets.

Raphaela, Mizzy, and Anne Marie hurried down from the broadcast booth. Mizzy looked around for something to use for the play-by-play and found the end of a drinking straw that was just the right size. Raphaela quickly sketched Figaro's profile on a notepad to capture his best side.

Mouse families from the Forum and from the Great Outdoors filed into the arena. Some of the young mice in the crowd wanted to eat right away, but their mothers told them to wait for the victory feast after the game. The mouse fans were all in a party mood, and began to cheer for the game to begin.

Anne Marie sold copies of the *Mouse Hockey News* for one gram of cheese a sheet.

"Let's go, captain!" said Figaro.

"Before we begin," Benny the Bullet said, "let us recite the MHL Players' Creed."

The team stood in a straight line in front of Benny. Each mouse held his helmet reverently over his heart. The mice in the audience rose to their feet also.

They recited the Creed in unison.

"I will play my best.
I will not slash, trip, or board.
I will shake hands with my opponents, win or lose.
I will be a good loser.
I will not fight with the referee.
I will be a good sport.
I will not be a puck hog.
I will be a team player.
I will never be a quitter.
I will play for the glory of the Cheddar Cup."

Everyone sighed at the noble feelings that the Creed inspired in them.

"Are you all wearing your mouse-guards?" asked Benny. He looked sternly at the players, and they all nodded.

"Well, what are we waiting for?" he shouted. "Let's play hockey."

"Not so fast, squirt," rumbled a deep voice from the far dark corner of the ice.

Big Boris and several other Rink Rats bobbed and tripped over the ice. They were wearing makeshift skates and suits of ragged underwear. Their homemade sticks seemed poorly put together.

"I told you we accepted your challenge

to play for the Cheddar Cup," sneered Big Boris. "You didn't think we were going to let you keep the Cup without a fight, did you?"

Benny recognized Old Scarface, Packer, and Sergeant. The others looked just as mean, except for one elderly rat who seemed slower on his feet. Benny could almost feel the Cheddar Cup slipping away from them again. Then he became angry.

"The Cup rightfully belongs to us," he told the Rink Rats. "But we'll play you for it. Fair and square."

"Fair and square," echoed Big Boris. His mouth curved in a wicked grin. "Why not? If that's the way you want it, then that's the way it's going to be. Right, boys?"

The Rink Rats nodded nervously.

"But I thought you said we could do anything we want to them, Boss," Packer stuttered. "I thought we could slash, bash, trip, grip, pound, pulverize..."

"Shut up, stupid," snapped Big Boris.

He turned once again to Benny the Bullet.

"Don't pay any attention to him," Big Boris told Benny with a snicker. "We've been standing around yakking long enough. Let's get started."

Benny stiffened. This would be the hardest task he and the other mice would ever have to face.

"We're ready," he said in a slow steady voice. "For anything."

## Chapter Fourteen

# THE BIG GAME

T HE mouse hockey players faced the Rink Rats at centre ice. The air was charged with electricity.

"We need a referee and two linemen," Benny demanded.

"Why bother?" Big Boris jeered. "Let's just play."

"No," said Benny firmly. "It wouldn't be fair."

"He's right, Boris," said the elderly rat who now skated forward. "Because of my age and experience, I'll be the referee. I remember some of the rules."

"Then we want two mice as linemen," insisted Peppy. "Two mice equal one rat...or something like that."

Two mouse hockey players named Monday and Friday volunteered. Three whistles were found for the officials. From each side a goal judge was chosen. The Rink Rats whacked their sticks on the ice to begin the game.

The referee dropped the puck in the face-off zone between the two centres, Figaro the Flyer and Sergeant. He blew his whistle.

The game was under way.

Sergeant smacked at the puck and smashed it across the blue line. It was stopped short by the Russian import Malenky. He passed to Squeaker, who tried to stickhandle around Packer. Packer sprawled on the ice. He jabbed his stick in the path of Squeaker, who went flying over the top of the stick and slammed into the boards.

Benny the Bullet scooped up the puck and skated for the opposite net. He faked to the right, then to the left, around a Rink Rat defenceman. The defenceman leaned too far forward and lost his balance. He crashed to the ice. Out of the corner of his eye, the Bullet saw Figaro come flying in on his right. He passed the puck, and Figaro made a driving shot on net. Old Scarface, the goaltender, came out of the net. He flicked the puck off his stick towards centre ice. The Big M shot the puck back. The Bullet picked up speed and skated for the puck.

Packer, the Rink Rat right winger, beat

him to it. He bashed the puck with his stick and sent it spinning down to the MHL zone. Sergeant and Big Boris charged after it. They collided at mid-ice, and then rubbed their sore heads. The mouse crowd cheered.

"I had it, Boss," cried Packer. "It was mine."

"It was my puck, stupid," snarled Big Boris.

Elated, the Bullet zoomed past them with Squeaker on his left. There was only one Rink Rat defenceman between him and the net. He passed the puck to Howie Squeaker, who was all alone. Squeaker took a shot on net, which just missed the corner. The Bullet scrabbled for the loose puck. He poked it out from under the nose of Sergeant, and then aimed a blistering shot on net. Old Scarface went down on all fours to stop the goal. The puck shot right through his open legs. The Mice had scored the first goal of the game.

Two mice marched out. They held up the score on a pair of empty match boxes, 1-0.

Big Boris was angry.

"We'll get you next time, squirt," he

muttered to Benny as they waited for the face-off.

By this time, Benny had forgotten his fear of the powerful Rink Rats. All that mattered was that he was playing hockey, the one thing in the world he would rather do than anything else.

The Rink Rats picked up the puck at centre ice in a breakaway. Big Boris and Packer streaked down the ice with it. Big Boris stumbled, but managed to stay on his skates as he hogged the puck. Packer cut in front of the net, and then skated through the goal crease. He sent Peppy sprawling on the seat of his pants. Just then, Big Boris let go a booming slap shot from the point and scored. The score was tied at 1-1. The goal judge blinked his pocket flashlight off and on to signal the goal.

"No fair!" Peppy protested, coming out of the net. "No rats allowed in the goal crease."

"Who do you think you are?" demanded Big Boris. "Ken Dryden?"

"Well, you're no Guy Lafleur yourself," muttered Peppy.

But it was too late. The old referee hadn't seen it, and had already signalled a goal.

"Don't worry team." Benny tried to brighten their spirits. "We'll get it back. The only way they can score is by cheating."

Figaro won the face-off and shot the puck across to the Bullet. Big Boris was waiting. The Bullet could see him coming, stick held high. He shot the puck over to Squeaker, but just as it left his stick, he felt Big Boris crash into him. The breath left Benny's body as he crashed into the boards. As his helmet hit, he saw little shooting pinpoints of light.

Friday blew his whistle. He made wild motions with his paws.

"Tripping, boarding, charging!" he shouted. "Rough play."

Benny's teammates skated over. He lay on the ice, out cold.

"Speak to us, captain," Figaro begged. "We can't lose you now."

"The Cheddar Cup is at stake," said the Big M. He bent over and gently rubbed Benny's chest.

Slowly Benny's eyes fluttered open. The shooting lights seemed to have gone away. He saw worried mouse faces staring down at him.

*"Mon Dieu!"* Peppy exclaimed. "I thought you were a goner."

"What happened?" murmured Benny. Slowly, painfully, he stood up and dusted the ice from the seat of his pants. He shook his head twice.

"Are you all right, captain?" asked Squeaker as Big Boris slowly skated over to the penalty box.

"Better than all right," said Benny firmly. "Listen, team! Those Rink Rats can't keep up with us. They're just a bunch of bush leaguers."

"What they lack in finesse," said Figaro, "they make up for in size. And brutality."

"We knew they'd play dirty," Benny agreed. "Our only chance is to outsmart them and skate rings around them."

With Big Boris in the penalty box, the Rink Rats played an even dirtier game than before. They hooked, tripped, slashed, and bashed. At times it seemed as though the puck was glued to their sticks. Peppy managed to stop all shots on net. So did Old Scarface. The second and third lines couldn't score either.

By the end of the second period Packer was skating on his ankles. Sergeant puffed and wheezed like an old train. Big Boris was hanging onto the boards. The Rat defencemen were in bad shape, too, hobbling back and forth on the ice, knees buckling.

"They can't skate for beans," Benny cried. He and the others were heading over to their bench between periods. "We're just too fast for them. And they're out of shape."

"It's only the end of the second period," said the Big M. "Can we hold them for another twenty minutes?"

"Think positive!" Benny said. "That's an order. Of course we can hold them."

On the bench, he passed along a juicy wedge of orange he had been saving for the team. The Rink Rats lit up a cigar butt and passed it along their bench. Benny rubbed his bruised legs.

The Cheddar Cup—what was to become of it? Could they count on the Rink Rats running out of steam? Benny looked over at them. They were hanging on the ropes. But then he couldn't remember ever feeling so tired either.

One more period to go.

# Chapter Fifteen

# THE CHEDDAR CUP

DURING intermission, Anne Marie scurried over to the mouse hockey players' bench.

"I've something important to tell you, captain," she whispered. Benny nodded, and the white mouse continued. "The Rink Rats are going to use chewing gum on their sticks. I overheard them talking just now."

"The dirty rats!" Benny said angrily. "They can't win fair and square so they have to play dirty."

He wracked his brain trying to come up with a plan—a counter attack. Then he remembered an important rule. Benny skated over to the old referee before he blew the whistle.

"Hold it!" Benny said.

The whistle fell out of the old referee's mouth.

"What for?" he asked.

"Stick inspection," said Benny. "We

have a right to inspect Big Boris's stick. No chewing gum allowed on equipment." He pointed to the Rat's blade. "There's gum stuck to his stick. I can see if from here."

The other mouse hockey players swarmed around Benny.

"Why, that's against the rules," said the old referee. "The Rink Rats wouldn't stoop to a trick like that. They're bigger and stronger than you little fellows."

"We have a right to ask for stick inspection," said Peppy.

"Whenever Big Boris gets the puck, it will automatically stick to his blade," said the Big M. "We'll never get the puck away from him."

The old referee spread his arms.

"All right, all right. I've heard enough."

He motioned for the Rink Rats to line up. He skated up to them and slowly knelt to inspect their sticks. His fingers ran along the wide curved stick blade that belonged to Big Boris. He held up a piece of chewing gum as big as the puck.

"Well, I declare," said the referee. "The little fellows are right." He shook his head sadly. "What's the world coming to?"

"Well, what are you going to do about it?" demanded Peppy. "Give him a penalty."

"The Rats automatically lose the game," said the Big M.

"Not so fast," said the old referee. He pointed at Big Boris and then at the penalty box. "Two minutes!"

Big Boris was furious.

"I'll get you for this, fink," he warned Benny as he skated past to the penalty box. He gave him a shove.

Benny trembled but he stood his ground.

"Boris's stick also has too wide a curve on it," he said, but the only one listening was Anne Marie. "You can put that in your paper, too," he told the white mouse as she wrote in her notebook. "And thanks for tipping us off."

"It's part of my job," she said. "Now, get out there and win that Cheddar Cup."

The mouse hockey players tried every trick they knew to score during the third period of the game. The puck passed back and forth between the Rink Rats and the Mice at a feverish pace. Most of the time, play was inside the Rink Rats' zone. Old Scarface was good behind the net even though he was on his knees or the seat of his underwear more often than standing up.

Finally, with only minutes left on the stopwatch, Big Boris planted himself squarely in front of the MHL goal. The Big M tried to check Packer's wild slap shot, but it was too high. The puck grazed the crossbar and then fell in front of the net. Big Boris kicked the rubber with his skate. Sergeant barrelled in, skidded into Peppy, and knocked him flat. The puck slid in on the right side of the net past Peppy. He skated out of the crease to the referee.

"You can't do that," screamed Benny the Bullet, skating over. "You can't score a goal with your skate. You have to use a stick."

"Says who?" demanded Big Boris. "I'll use my stick on your head, you little squirt."

Big Boris dropped his stick and gloves. He skated over to Benny and doubled his paws into fists. Benny stood up to him, nose to nose.

"He kicked it in with his foot," cried Peppy.

Peppy circled around the referee. Sergeant gave Peppy a shove, and Peppy shoved him back.

"No goal! No goal!" cried the old referee who skated slowly over. "You have to use a stick—not your skate."

The linesmen, Monday and Friday, skated over to break up the scuffling players. The cheers from the onlookers were louder than the jeers. In the crowd, the rats were outnumbered fifty to one.

"Let's get them, team," Benny muttered. "The score is still tied at 1-all."

Figaro and Sergeant faced off in the MHL zone. The timekeeper held up his stopwatch to signal one minute to go as the puck dropped between them.

Quickly Figaro slapped Sergeant's stick and got the shot away. Squeaker passed to the Bullet. He picked the puck up at the blue line and stickhandled around a Rat defenceman. He passed to Squeaker, who ducked under a vicious crosscheck from Big Boris. Squeaker fired a shot on goal, but Old Scarface fell on it, face first. He stopped the puck! There was one more scar on his face when he stood up. A fresh red welt.

"That's it, squirts," jeered the goaltender. He wiped his face on the sleeve of his underwear. "You'll be sorry you ever challenged us for the Cheddar Cup."

"Says who?" yelled the Big M as he skated past.

"Says me," Old Scarface answered. "I'm going to keep right on nailing you until that big hunk of cheese is ours."

Benny fumed. The Rink Rats had no respect for the Cup. No respect at all.

Time was running out as the two centre forwards faced off in the Rink Rats' zone. Sergeant bashed the puck and sent it spinning across centre ice. A Rat defenceman reached the puck and shot it into the corner. There was a mad scramble for it in the MHL zone. Figaro grabbed the puck. He sang as he skated across the blue line:

"Toreador-a
This is how we score
We just need one more
We'll show 'em how to score."

Sneakily, Sergeant poked his stick at Figaro from behind. Figaro locked the stick blade tightly under his arm. He lost the puck as the tired Rink Rat held tightly to the other end of the stick. Then Sergeant did the splits as he stumbled and crashed into an oncoming defenceman.

Benny scooped up the loose puck around centre ice. He knew that the easiest player to stickhandle around is the one who rushes straight at you. And Big Boris was heading straight for him. Benny waited until the last split second before sliding the puck through the legs of Big Boris. Then he skated quickly around him. The Big M caught it and passed back to Benny. Big Boris continued to coast until he hit the boards with a crash that shook the glass.

The Bullet crossed the red line. With a flick of his wrist, he flipped the puck high towards the rafters. Everyone looked up as the puck lifted several metres into the air. It bounced on its edge in front of the goalkeeper. Benny looked dumbfounded as old Scarface sprawled in front of the goal. The puck bounced over his shoulder into the net. The goal judge blinked his pocket flashlight on and off to signal a goal.

Benny had broken the tie game! The score was 2-1 for the MHL. The crowd was in an uproar as the timekeeper signalled the end of the game. The scorekeepers ran out to carry the score boxes around the rink, MHL-2, Rink Rats-1.

"We did it! We did it!" Everyone shouted at once. "We beat the Rink Rats."

"The Cup is ours to keep."

The players skated over to the goal and jumped on Peppy. They pulled off his face mask and helmet, and rubbed his ears. Then the mouse hockey players piled on top of one another, pulling off helmets, whacking each other on the back, celebrating their victory. Someone grabbed Benny's silver helmet and threw it into the crowd for a souvenir. A small white mouse caught it.

"We've got to shake hands with the Rink Rats," Benny said. "Win or lose, remember?"

There were a few groans, but gradually the players lined up behind their captain. He skated over to the Rink Rats.

Big Boris was busy protesting the game to the referee.

"I thought you were on our side," he said to the old rat.

"Game over!" ruled the referee, waving his arms for silence. "And a good thing too. Disgraceful. A spectacle. Not sport at all. Not like the good old days. Letting those little fellows skate rings around you."

"Sorry," said Benny, skating up to Big Boris. "Better luck next time."

"What next time?" sneered Big Boris. He shook Benny's arm away.

"We'll put the Cup away until next year," said Benny. "After the victory celebration."

"Hope it rots," muttered Big Boris. "Come on, gang."

He shambled off towards the far dark corner at the end of the rink. The other Rink Rats followed slowly, limping and hobbling, knees buckling, ankles wobbling. Their old underwear uniforms hung in shreds.

The minute the Rink Rats disappeared, it was as if a heavy dark cloud had lifted.

The mouse hockey fans swarmed onto the ice to congratulate the players.

Then came the moment everyone had been waiting for. The mice rolled the Cheddar Cup out to the ice. A red knitted scarf was unrolled in front of it. Benny the Bullet, as captain, accepted the Cup with pride. Benny and his teammates skated around the ice pushing the Cup ahead of them.

The beautiful waxen Cup was filled to overflowing with cheese. The cheese had been brought into the Forum by the mice—Edam, Gouda, Brie, Camembert, Roquefort, Limburger, and Cheddar.

"Well, what are we waiting for?" Benny cried. "Dig in!"

At his words, the mice scrambled over the Cheddar Cup. They climbed inside, broke off bits of the cheeses inside, and threw them at each other. Someone rubbed Peppy's face in a wedge of Camambert cheese. Figaro dug into a chunk of Gouda.

The celebration lasted all night long and into the small hours of the morning. They danced and ate and talked endlessly about the game. Anne Marie sold copies of the *Mouse Hockey News*. Raphaela very artistically gnawed the champions' names onto the base of the Cup. Missy Mouse explained some of the finer points of the game to the fans.

In the midst of the celebration, Benny noticed that the Big M had hardly eaten a thing. He had packed his belongings into a piece of red cloth and tied the bag to the end of his hockey stick. As he headed for the gate, Benny rushed over.

"Where are you going?" he demanded.

The Big M stopped, scraped his feet on

the ice, and looked embarrassed.

"Home," he said.

"Back to the dump?"

The Big M nodded.

"But why?" asked Benny, surprised. "I thought you wanted to be a hockey player."

"I *am* a hockey player," said the Big M, "and I always *will* be a hockey player."

"Then why are you leaving?"

"I miss the food and the fresh air, I guess," said the Big M. He put his spectacles back on. "There's nothing wrong with the food here, Benny. A change in diet is good. But I miss my peanut butter sandwiches and fresh fruit. I miss the cookouts over an open fire most of all. And the moon and the stars overhead. I miss them, too."

"Thanks for everything," Benny said softly. Suddenly he could hardly speak. "We wouldn't have won the Cup without you on our team."

"Good-bye, Benny!" The Big M walked to the door by the garbage bin, turned, and waved. And then he was gone.

Benny's heart suddenly felt empty, as if a piece of it were missing.

Maybe it was time for a change, he

thought. Maybe he and Peppy and Figaro could visit the dump in the summer for a little holiday. Figaro had been begging him to go for a short vacation to the new opera house.

Suddenly Benny felt happy again as he returned to the victory celebration. You couldn't keep a good hockey player down once he had played in the big league. The MHL was in Benny's blood. And somehow he knew that he would be seeing the Big M again—one way or another.

The MHL was in his blood now, too.

# About the Author

Estelle Salata is an ex-hockey-mother who lives in Hamilton, Ontario. Her writing has been published in a number of magazines and anthologies for both children and adults. Several of her stories have been about hockey, inspired by her family's interest. One day an artist friend sent her a drawing of a mouse wearing a walnut shell hockey helmet and safety pin skates. The drawing appealed to Estelle's imagination, and *Mice at Centre Ice* was born. The novel has been made into an animated television special.

# Titles in the Series